Kylie Jean

Singing Queen

by Marci Peschke

illustrated by Tuesday Mourning

PICTURE WINDOW BOOKS
a capstone imprint

Kylie Jean is published by Picture Window Books
A Capstone Imprint
1710 Roe Crest Drive
North Mankato, Minnesota 56003
www.capstonepub.com

Library of Congress Cataloging-in-Publication Data
Peschke, M. (Marci)
  Singing queen / by Marci Peschke ; illustrated by Tuesday Mourning.
      p. cm. -- (Kylie Jean)
  Summary: Kylie Jean shows her talent for singing at the annual Jubilee Talent
Show.
  ISBN 978-1-4048-6800-7 (library binding) -- ISBN 978-1-4048-7211-0 (pbk.)
  ISBN 978-1-4048-7615-6 (pbk.)
  1. Fourth of July--Juvenile fiction. 2. Fourth of July celebrations--Juvenile fiction.
3. Talent shows--Juvenile fiction. 4. Singing--Juvenile fiction. 5. Texas--Juvenile
fiction. [1. Fourth of July--Fiction. 2. Talent shows--Fiction. 3. Singing--Fiction. 4.
Texas--Fiction.] I. Mourning, Tuesday, ill. II. Title.
  PZ7.P441245Si 2012
  813.6--dc23   2011029705

Creative Director: Heather Kindseth
Graphic Designer: Emily Harris
Editor: Beth Brezenoff
Production Specialist: Danielle Ceminsky

Design Element Credit:
Shutterstock/blue67design

Printed in the United States of America in North Mankato, Minnesota.
122012   007102R

Dedicated to Ana
with love for Rick

—MP

Table of Contents

All About Me, Kylie Jean!

My name is Kylie Jean Carter. I live in a big, sunny, yellow house on Peachtree Lane in Jacksonville, Texas with Momma, Daddy, and my two brothers, T.J. and Ugly Brother.

T.J. is my older brother, and Ugly Brother is . . . well . . . he's really a dog. Don't you go telling him he is a dog. Okay? I mean it. He thinks he is a real true person.

He is a black-and-white bulldog. His front looks like his back, all smashed in. His face is all droopy like he's sad, but he's not.

His two front teeth stick out, and his tongue hangs down. (Now you know why his name is Ugly Brother.)

Everyone I love to the moon and back lives in Jacksonville. Nanny, Pa, Granny, Pappy, my aunts, my uncles, and my cousins all live here. I'm extra lucky, because I can see all of them any time I want to!

My momma says I'm pretty. She says I have eyes as blue as the summer sky and a smile as sweet as an angel. (Momma says pretty is as pretty does. That means being nice to the old folks, taking care of little animals, and respecting my momma and daddy.)

But I'm pretty on the outside and on the inside. My hair is long, brown, and curly.

I wear it in a ponytail sometimes, but my absolute most favorite is when Momma pulls it back in a princess style on special days.

I just gave you a little hint about my big dream. Ever since I was a bitty baby I have wanted to be an honest-to-goodness beauty queen. I even know the wave. It's side to side, nice and slow, with a dazzling smile. I practice all the time, because everybody knows beauty queens need to have a perfect wave.

I'm Kylie Jean, and I'm going to be a beauty queen. Just you wait and see!

Chapter One

Summertime

Early in the morning, the sun is already hot as a firecracker when Momma's van pulls up in front of a tiny brick building.

I'm wearing my old red and white striped one-piece swimsuit. That's because today, Momma is letting me swim at the city pool with my friend Cara.

It only costs a dollar to get in for the whole day! Can you believe it?

Before I get out, Momma turns around in the front seat. "Did you bring a towel and sunscreen in your bag? How about change for snacks?" she asks.

I hold up the beach bag covered in pink and white anchors and answer, "Yes, ma'am. And I have some quarters from my piggy bank."

"You better be good and do what the lifeguard tells you. You hear?" Momma tells me.

"Don't worry," I say. "I'll be good, Momma." Then I climb out of the van, dragging my bag along with me to the sidewalk. I slip off my flip-flops and pretend I'm walking on hot coals like they do at the circus.

At the window, I pay my dollar to get in. Then I shove open the big metal gate.

As soon as I walk through, I see the pool! It's a giant circle of water the color of bright blue Jell-O.

I start looking for Cara right off. She's not in one of the long chairs. Those are filled with older girls trying to get a tan. There's a tall chair with a lifeguard.

I know him. His name is Wes. He's my brother T.J.'s friend, and he makes you follow the pool rules.

Right in front of the lifeguard's stand is a tiny round baby pool. Mommies sit all along the edge holding their little kids. The babies kick their legs while the mommies talk.

I see Cara in the shallow end of the pool. She waves and shouts, "Hey, Kylie Jean, I'm over here!"

I jump into the pool. The warm water laps against my face as I swim over to Cara. "Let's play mermaid!" she says.

First, I pretend to swish my long mermaid tail. Really, it's just my legs twisted together. Then Cara swishes her tail too.

After a while, I climb out of the pool and stand on the edge.

I yell, "Look at me! Cannonball!"

I take three giant steps back. Then I run toward the pool. As I jump into the deep end, I tuck myself into a tiny ball.

Whoosh!

Water splashes everywhere. It rains fat little drops all over the older girls sunbathing in their bikinis.

"I'll never get a good tan if you keep on getting me wet!" one of them yells.

"No more cannonballs!" another one says.

I dog paddle over to Cara, and we both laugh. She gives me a high five.

Then she says, "That was your best one yet! If your splash was any bigger you'd hit the lifeguard and get in trouble."

I nod. "He'd tell T.J. and T.J. would tell Momma," I say. Then I have a really great idea of something fun we can do at the pool.

"Hey, you wanna dive for quarters?" I ask.

"Sure!" Cara says.

I run over to my pool bag and find some of my shiny new quarters. Then I hop back into the water — no cannonball this time — and hang on to the side of the pool.

I drop the coins.

Cara says, "Ready . . . set . . . go!"

We dive in.

The coins spiral down through the blue water like shiny fish bait. Wiggling through the water like tadpoles, we swim after the silvery treasure. After a minute, Cara swims up for air. I do too. Then we dive back down and finally find the quarters.

Afterward, we float on our backs for a while.

"I love summertime," I say.

"Me too," Cara says. Then she asks, "Hey! Are you goin' to the Fourth of July Jubilee on Saturday?"

"Yup!" I say. "We always do. Granny is makin' jewelry for the craft show, and Momma always makes a real big picnic for my whole family to eat. I love the Jubilee!"

"Me too," Cara says. "I just love summer."

"I do too," I tell her.

"They're havin' a talent show this year at the Jubilee," Cara tells me. "It's gonna be just like American Idol, but not as big, since only folks from our town will be in it."

Right then, an idea hits my brain like ketchup on French fries!

I bet I could do a talent in the talent show!

"How old do you have to be to be in the show?" I ask.

Cara shrugs. "I dunno," she says. "Nobody told me any of the rules."

My mind is spinning faster than a fan blade on a hot August day.

I like the pool, but I have work to do now!

I swim to the side of the pool and climb out, dripping water as I walk over to my pink towel and my beach bag.

"I gotta go home now," I tell Cara. "Are you coming to the pool tomorrow?"

She laughs and splashes some water at me. "Yes," she says. "I'm going to come every day until school starts again, unless it's raining. See you tomorrow!"

Waving goodbye, I drag my pool bag and pink towel to the pool gate.

Chapter Two
Big News

I run home as fast as I can, dragging my big ole beach bag behind me. I speed down the street and take a shortcut through Granny and Pappy's yard. They won't mind.

The air smells like green grass. Pappy is out mowing the lawn.

"How's my girl?" he shouts when he sees me.

I just wave back. I don't have time to stop and chat.

I have to concentrate on how I can find out about the contest.

When I pass Miss Clarabelle's driveway, I see her newspaper lying on the ground. This gives me an idea! Newspapers have lots of things in them, and I bet one of the things in this newspaper is the rules about the talent show at the Fourth of July Jubilee.

When I run up our driveway, Ugly Brother and the paper are both waiting for me.

"Can you help me find out about the Jubilee?" I ask Ugly Brother.

He runs over to me and barks, "Ruff, ruff!"

Two barks means yes!

"Thanks, Ugly Brother," I say.

Together, we sit in the grass under the shade of a big oak tree and look at the newspaper.

"Do you think I can find out about the Jubilee in the paper?" I ask Ugly Brother.

He barks, "Ruff, ruff." Two barks again! Ugly Brother and I are on the right track.

I tear the plastic wrapper off of the paper. Then a breeze blows the paper open.

When I look up, I notice that the sky is gray. It looks like it might rain. The pages of the newspaper keep flipping in the wind. Ugly Brother decides to help me out by standing on one side of the paper while I look at the other side.

Before I look for the Jubilee, I read the comics. Those comics are so funny! Ugly Brother likes the one with the big orange cat who eats everything. That's his favorite. My favorite is one with a lot of kids who live in a house and like to run all over their neighborhoods all the time.

We are busy laughing together when it starts to rain.

There is a teeny tiny clap of thunder. Then it's like a river falls out of the sky and we both get soaking wet.

I take off for the porch, yelling, "Hurry, Ugly Brother! The paper will get wet!"

He follows me, dragging my pool bag and towel. He is not a very fast runner like me.

It's too late to save the paper. The pages are a damp smudgy mess.

I sit down on the porch floor. Ugly Brother plops down right next to me.

"I guess we'll need a new plan," I say.

My daddy works at the newspaper. Maybe he'll bring me home a new copy.

"Should I call Daddy?" I ask Ugly Brother. "I just know he could bring me the newspaper when he comes home from work. Right?"

Ugly Brother turns his head to the side and barks, "Ruff!"

One bark means no. "You're right," I say. "That's way too long to wait. Daddy won't be home from work until five-thirty."

I think about it for a while longer while the rain falls down outside.

The answer hits my brain like rain on a polka-dotted umbrella. Granny will know all about the rules. Granny knows about everything for the Jubilee.

I run into the house and straight to the phone in the kitchen.

I dial Granny's number. I know it by heart. Granny answers. She knows it's me as soon as I say hello.

"Hello, Kylie Jean. What are you doing today?" asks Granny.

"Oh, I went to the pool with Cara this morning," I tell her.

"That sounds fun," Granny says. "Today was a good day for the pool, before it started raining. Nice and hot out. What did you do with your friend?"

"We dove for quarters and played mermaid," I say. "And she told me they're putting on a talent show at the Jubilee this year."

"That's right, they sure are!" Granny says. "It should be a great show."

"Can you tell me all about the contest? Pretty please?" I say. "I know you'll be at the Jubilee craft show selling your jewelry."

Granny laughs. She says, "You can just go right on down to Jacksonville City Hall and sign up for the show."

"Only if they let kids sign up," I say.

"That's right, darlin'," Granny says.

"Do you know if they do?" I ask nervously. "Cara didn't know if kids could be in it."

"Hmm," Granny says. "Well, I just don't know. I hope so, because you sure are a talented little girl, and I'd love to see you in the Jubilee talent show. Miss June at City Hall will know all of the rules."

"Thanks, Granny," I say. "I better get moving!"

After I hang up, I look at Ugly Brother. "That was just the first part of my plan," I tell him. "We need to get an umbrella and take a walk for part two."

He barks twice. Ugly Brother likes this plan.

My big umbrella is right by the front door. I step outside and pop it open. Ugly Brother is still waiting inside. He doesn't like getting wet.

"Come on," I say. "I got the big umbrella so we both can fit under it."

"Ruff, ruff!" Ugly Brother says. Then the two of us head off down the street under the giant umbrella.

Chapter Three
City Hall Sign Up

On our way to City Hall, the rain stops.
Right away, it starts to get hot out. Real hot. I'm
sweating inside my rubber boots and raincoat, so
we stop to get a Sno-ball.

The roof on the Sno-ball stand looks like a huge
rainbow-flavored Sno-ball. Inside the Sno-ball
there is only room for one person.

Ugly Brother and I stand in line, waiting for our
turn. It's a long line. I count the people in front of
us.

One, two, three, four, five, six. We have a long time to wait!

The first person in line orders a lemon twist Sno-ball. The next two people order rainbow-flavored Sno-balls. I don't hear the rest because I am too busy talking to Ugly Brother.

I ask him, "Do you want your usual flavor?"

He barks, "Ruff, ruff."

"Okay. Grape for you and cotton candy for me," I say.

When it's our turn, I order. The teenage boy who's working hands me one pink and one purple Sno-ball. I pay with some quarters from my pocket.

I put the purple Sno-ball on the ground for Ugly Brother. He slurps and grunts, enjoying the frozen treat. The pink one is for me.

We start walking.

My tongue is pink, but Ugly Brother's is purple like a grape. The Sno-ball is nice and cold. It feels good in the heat.

I have one bite left as we walk up to City Hall. City Hall isn't really a hall, not like the hall in my house, anyway. It's really just a big ole white house downtown near the county courthouse.

I suck down the last sweet goodness of my cotton candy Sno-ball. Then I tie Ugly Brother up to the bicycle stand right in front of Jacksonville City Hall.

"You be good and no barking. Okay?" I tell him. He whines and sits down. I know he wants to come with me, but most places don't let dogs come inside. I don't know why.

Inside City Hall, the air is ice cold. My boots squish across the floor all the way over to Miss June's desk. Squish, squish, squish.

I look behind me and see that I'm leaving some wet footprints on the floor. I hope that Miss June doesn't mind!

Miss June hears me coming and looks up.

"Well, hello there!" she says. "How are you doing, Kylie Jean?" she asks. "And how about your big brother and your momma and daddy? Are you gettin' excited for the Jubilee?"

"Yes ma'am, I am," I say. "And we're all fine, thank you." Then I ask, "I need some help. How old do you have to be to sign up for the Jubilee talent show?"

Miss June doesn't say anything. Instead, she offers me a red and white striped peppermint stick from her candy jar.

I remember my manners and say, "Thank you, ma'am."

She says, "You're welcome. I need to make a quick call to find out the answer to your question. Okay?"

"Yes ma'am," I say.

Miss June punches a number into the phone and starts talking real quietly.

I snap the candy stick in half. Pop!

I'm saving part of it for Ugly Brother as a treat for being good outside while he waits for me.

After a long time, Miss June finally hangs up the phone.

"It seems we didn't really put anything in the rules about age," she tells me. "If you are old enough to have talent, you're in."

She hands me a clipboard.

Then she adds, "Good thing you came today since it's the last day to sign up. Just write your name, talent, and how long you'll be on the stage."

I bite my lip. Then I admit, "I'm not sure just yet what I'll be doing or for how long."

Miss June smiles. She says, "Just put down your name for now."

"All right," I say. "I'll be back tomorrow to put down the rest."

Then I head back outside, my boots squishing against the floor.

Outside, the sky is bright blue and it seems even hotter than before. Pa always says in Texas it can rain one minute and shine the next.

Ugly Brother has wiggled loose to look in the window for me. What a naughty boy!

I throw up my hands. "Ugly Brother, I brought you half my candy and here you are being a bad boy!" I say, grabbing his collar. "I told you to stay where I put you!"

He looks a little sad.

"Next time I tell you to stay, you better stay, or no candy for you. Okay? You got it, mister? And I mean it!" I say. Then I hand him his half of my candy stick.

He barks twice as he chomps down the candy stick in one bite. Then I tell him all about what Miss June said.

Ugly Brother seems excited, but I'm starting to get nervous.

Tomorrow I have to decide on my talent.

As we walk home, I make a list in my head.

There are lots of things I can do. I can think of a whole bunch of talents.

I can dance.

I can twirl a baton.

I can do a real good beauty-queen wave.

I can hop on one foot for a really long time, and I can turn cartwheels.

I can paint real pretty pictures.

I could read poetry or act or sing or do doggie tricks.

That last one might not work, since Ugly Brother would be the talented one, and his name isn't on the list. I didn't even think to ask if dogs are allowed in the talent show.

Besides, sometimes Ugly Brother is just too lazy to be talented!

I decide to go across the street and play with Cole and think about my talent later. Sometimes resting your brain makes it think better.

Chapter Four

Sing or Dance?

After thinking about my talent all night, I decide I should do either singing or dancing. But I need another opinion.

Momma always says two heads are better than one. So after I swim at the pool with Cara and my best cousin, Lucy, I stop by Granny and Pappy's house.

When I walk into their big blue house, I see that Pappy is in his La-Z-Boy chair watching golf on TV.

"Granny's on the sun-porch," he says. "You go on back and find her, sugar."

On the sun-porch, Granny has boxes and boxes of beads in every color on a long table. They are so pretty! They look like candy.

"Hello, Kylie Jean!" Granny says. "Have a seat."

I sit down and look at the beads. Granny asks, "Did you come to help me make jewelry for the Jubilee?"

"Sort of," I say. Then I hold up a handful of sparkly beads that look like diamonds. "I love this bling!" I tell Granny. "I'll help you, and you can help me."

Granny smiles. "All right," she says. "What do you need help with?"

"I need help decidin'. Should I sing or dance at the talent show?" I ask.

Granny keeps working on a necklace. It has strands of red beads and white beads. They look just like red and white stripes in her lap. I start working too. I'm planning on making a blingy bracelet.

Granny says, "I think you should sing."

"But what song?" I ask.

Granny thinks for a while.

Then she smiles and says, "The Star-Spangled Banner would be just perfect."

I get excited! I shout, "That's a great idea. I just gotta learn all the words by heart!" Then I add, "I better go tell Miss June right now."

"Be careful!" Granny yells as I dash toward the back door.

"Okay!" I yell back. Then I start running.

I skip all the way down to City Hall. My flip-flops squeak over the floor as I walk to Miss June's desk.

She smiles when she sees me coming and asks, "You're back! Did you figure out your talent?"

"Yes ma'am," I say. "I'm singing The Star-Spangled Banner!"

Chapter Five

Stars and Stripes Singer

When I wake up on Wednesday, I realize that I only have a few days to learn my song for the talent show.

I throw off the covers and scoot out of bed. Ugly Brother whines and sticks his nose farther under my blankets. He's not ready to get up. But the Jubilee is on Saturday, so we have to get going.

"You better get up or you can't go with me to the library after breakfast," I warn him.

He rolls over and jumps sleepily off the bed while I get dressed in my red and white striped sundress. I brush my hair. Then I brush my teeth.

Downstairs in the kitchen, I fix my own breakfast. First I get a bowl and a spoon. Next I have to choose my cereal. I like Fruity Rings and Chocolate Toasty Os. I hold up both of the boxes.

"Which one?" I ask.

Ugly Brother jumps up, trying to lick the box of Fruity Rings.

"How did you know which cereal I wanted?" I ask happily.

I sprinkle a couple of Fruity Rings on the floor for him to eat. Crunch. Crunch. Crunch.

Then I pour some in my bowl. Before I can get the milk out, T.J. comes in. He pours some Chocolate Toasty Os in Momma's biggest mixing bowl.

"Are you mowing lawns today?" I ask him while he pours milk into his bowl.

T.J.'s lawn-mowing business really keeps him busy in the summer. He mows lawns for Mrs. Bates, the Parkers, Miss Clarabelle, Daddy's boss at the paper, and the Millers.

"Yep. I have a few to mow today," he tells me, eating fast. "What are you going to do today?"

"I'm going to the library to get a book of songs, so I can learn my song for the Jubilee talent show," I say.

T.J. shoves the last bite of cereal in his mouth. Then he winks and says, "Pick a good one, so you can win it." He puts on his Texas Rangers cap and scoots out the door.

As soon as I finish my Fruity Rings, I head on over to the library. Ugly Brother comes along. We take our time walking slowly along Peach Tree Lane.

When we turn down Main Street, I wave at the mailman and the old men sitting in front of the barbershop. Then we stop right in front of the library.

"Sit! You stay right here," I tell Ugly Brother.

He barks, "Ruff, ruff."

I head inside.

When I ring the little bell on the checkout counter, Ms. Patrick, the librarian, hurries over. She asks, "What are you up to now, Kylie Jean?"

"I need the words to The Star-Spangled Banner," I tell her. "The book I get has to have all of the words. Can you please help me? Do you have a songbook like that?"

Ms. Patrick nods. "Follow me," she says.

She stops in front of one shelf and pulls out a picture book. I take it and start turning through the pages. It's cool, but the words are too spread out.

I hand it back, shaking my head. "I sure am sorry, ma'am, but I need the words all on one page. This book has a little of the words on each page."

Ms. Patrick slides the book back on the shelf. Then she whispers, "Follow me. I have just the book you're looking for."

When she hands me the next book, it is just what I need! All the words are on one page in the back of the book. "This is perfect," I tell her.

After I check out the book with my library card, I go outside and sit on the library steps. Ugly Brother and I look at the words to the song.

There are four verses. I know the first one, but in the other three, the words are really big ones to learn by heart.

Then an idea hits my brain like ants at picnic. I can just sing the first verse three times.

We go straight home without waving to anyone, so I can start to practice my song.

I sing it while I help Momma fold the towels. Then I sing it while I help Miss Clarabelle weed the flower beds. She sings with me, too!

Later I sing all the way to the pool. While we swim, my friends listen to me sing it over and over. Soon they're singing it too.

When I get home, I head straight to my room to change.

I sing all the way up the stairs and while I'm putting my play clothes on. Ugly Brother sings, too.

Then someone bangs on my door. T.J. shouts, "I can't hear my music with all your howling!"

"Okay," I say. "Sorry!" But I whisper the song two more times.

After dinner, Daddy wants to hear my song. I sit in his lap to sing to him.

I tell him, "Just listen to me. I know all the words. You have to wait, cause I'm gonna sing it three times. Okay?"

Daddy gives me a big squeezy hug. "Okay, baby girl. Sing your song for me right now," he says.

I start singing. But it has been a long, busy day. The words to my song start to float away from me. Daddy kisses me on the cheek and carries me upstairs to bed. I am one sleepy little singer.

Chapter Six
Glitter Girl

The first thing I do on Thursday morning is call Cara. As soon as her momma gives her the phone, I say, "Can you skip swimming at the pool today? I need help me with my costume for the talent show."

"Sure. What kind of costume do you want?" she asks.

"I don't know," I admit. "All I know is I want a really good one!"

Cara giggles. Then she says, "Okay, tell me more when I get to your house. I'll come right over."

After we say goodbye and hang up, I head out to the front yard to wait for Cara. Ugly Brother waits too.

Before too long, Cara speeds up on her red racer bicycle.

We run inside and go upstairs to my bedroom. On the way up, I explain what I have in mind.

"I want something red, white, and blue, because I am singing a very patriotic song," I tell her.

"Do you have a white t-shirt and some red glitter?" she asks.

"Yes!" I say. The white shirt is in a drawer with my play clothes, so I pull it out.

While Cara waits, I dig around in my desk drawer for some red glitter.

She sits down on my bed. "Look for some glue, too, okay?" she says.

"Found it!" I shout, holding up the bottle of glue and the small jar of red glitter.

Cara spreads the t-shirt out on the floor so we can fix it up. She draws some stripes onto the shirt with a pencil.

I smear on the glue. Then Cara carefully shakes red glitter in between the pencil marks.

Ugly Brother wanders over to see what's going on. He tries to sniff my sparkly shirt. He gets the red glitter all over his nose.

"Don't you go sniffing glitter," I tell him. "Now you look like Rudolph the red-nosed reindeer!"

Cara and I laugh so hard we fall over on the floor. Ugly Brother is so silly!

Once we calm down, we put red glitter on my red flip-flops. There's glitter all over my room, sparkling on the floor.

Cara looks around and says, "With all this red glitter in your pink room, it looks like a Valentine's Day card."

"You're thinkin' about the wrong holiday! Remember, the Jubilee is a Fourth of July party," I reminder her.

Cara says, "I know, but I love pink and red together."

"What else should I wear?" I ask.

She thinks for a minute. Then she says, "It will be really hot outside. Are you gonna wear shorts?"

In the very bottom of one of my drawers, I find some blue shorts with white stars. "These will be perfect with my new sparkly top!" I exclaim.

"Do you want to borrow my headband with glittery blue stars on it?" Cara asks.

"Oh, yes! It will look so perfect with my costume," I reply.

Cara smiles. "You are going to be the only glitter girl in the talent show," she says.

I can't wait for the glue to dry so I can try on my glamorous glittery costume. But Cara can't wait to get back in the pool. She says, "I'm going to ride my bike over to the pool. Want to come?"

"Maybe later," I say. "But thanks for coming and helping me."

"You're welcome! See you later," she says. Then she waves and runs out of my room.

While I wait for the glue on my shirt and shoes to dry, I practice my song in front of my mirror. It is a tall oval mirror with a floor stand, and I can see all of me in it. I use a marker for a microphone. Then I sing my heart out.

I try to remember all the words and sing them nice and loud.

When I sing the song for the tenth time, Ugly Brother starts howling. I guess he's getting sick of my singing, but a singing queen needs her practice. I open my bedroom door and push him into the hall.

"Sorry, Ugly Brother," I say. "You better go downstairs if you don't want to listen to my beautiful singing anymore."

He doesn't argue or try to come back in my room. Instead he heads for the stairs. I slam my door and keep on singing.

After I sing the song about a hundred more times, I check my shirt. It is finally dry. Yippee!

I pull on my costume. Then I stand in front of my mirror.

Wow! I love my costume! When I get Cara's headband it will be perfect.

I race downstairs to show Momma and Ugly Brother. They are both in the kitchen.

"Look at my costume!" I exclaim.

Momma is surprised. "Wow!" she says. Then she asks, "Did you make it yourself?"

"Cara helped me make it," I say. "She's going to let me wear her blue headband with stars on it, too."

"That sounds perfect," Momma says.

Ugly Brother sniffs my leg.

Momma smiles. "Looks like Ugly Brother helped too," she says.

"How did you know?" I ask.

Momma points at Ugly Brother's nose. "His nose matches your costume," she says. Then she smiles again. "You and Cara are so creative. You're going to be a sparkly little star!"

Chapter Seven
Picnic Planning

On Friday morning, Momma and I get up
bright and early. It's our job to plan the family
Fourth of July picnic.

Momma wants to make a menu for our picnic
lunch. "What should we have with our fried
chicken?" she asks. "We have to have fried chicken
or it won't seem like the Jubilee!"

"How about deviled eggs?" I suggest.

Ugly Brother agrees. "Ruff, ruff," he barks.

Ugly Brother really likes eggs, any way you cook them. On Saturday mornings he eats them scrambled and on Sundays he eats them fried. I think he would eat eggs every single day if Momma would make them for him.

I like eggs too, but I only like the yellow gooey part of the egg. The white part tastes like rubber. That seems gross to me.

"All right," Momma says. "It's hard to beat your granny's deviled eggs, so it's a good thing I have her recipe."

No one makes better deviled eggs than Granny! I even eat the white part when it's one of Granny's deviled eggs.

"What else?" Momma asks.

We think and talk and plan. Our menu continues to fill up. Momma writes down that we'll make potato salad, homemade pickles, biscuits, pies, and brownies.

Then an idea hits my brain like a crust on a cherry pie.

"We need something cold to drink," I tell Momma. "How about making pink lemonade?"

She says, "That's a great idea! I'll put it on the menu, along with a jug of sweet tea."

At last, our menu is finished. Time to start cooking!

Momma puts on her apron. It has big bright red cherries on it. I put on my pink apron with the cute little strawberries on it. You know pink is my color!

Then we get to work.

First, we have to boil the eggs.

Momma pulls a chair over to the counter. I climb up and stand on it, carefully putting all of the eggs in the pan. I count each one as I put them in the water. "One, two, three, four, five, six, seven, eight, nine, ten, eleven, twelve," I say.

When I get to twelve, Momma says, "You don't have to count them all. Just hurry and get them in the pan so we can put them on the burner."

It takes a long time for water to boil. Momma warned me a long time ago that if you watch a pot it won't boil. The sooner it boils, the sooner I can make the deviled eggs, so I don't look at the pot one single time. I don't even peek.

Instead, I squeeze lemons for the lemonade. You need muscles to be good at squeezing them. T.J. is a better lemon squeezer, but he is mowing the Parkers' lawn. He likes to mow early before it gets too hot outside.

As I'm squeezing lemons, the pan lid pops off of the egg pot and white foamy bubbles rush out all over the stove!

Ugly Brother runs all around the kitchen, barking.

"Oh no!" Momma shouts. She grabs some paper towels.

"Maybe we should've watched that pot after all," I say quietly. Momma laughs.

When she gets everything cleaned up, we put the boiled eggs into a bowl with ice water to cool them down.

Momma sighs. "Well, my dear, I think that was enough kitchen excitement for today," she says. "Don't you think?"

I am too busy peeling off the hard white shells to answer. That's my favorite part of making deviled eggs.

I roll the eggs back and forth on the kitchen table to crack them. Then I pull long white ribbons of shell off of each cooked egg.

"You're doing great," Momma says. "I count seven peeled eggs already, and that's not an easy job."

"Thanks, Momma," I say. Peeling eggs doesn't seem like something a beauty queen would do, but I like it. "I guess I could be an egg-peeling queen," I add.

Momma laughs. "You sure could," she says. "You'd be the best egg-peeling queen the world has ever seen."

While I finish peeling eggs, Momma rolls out pie dough for her cherry cheesecake pie. She hums along as I sing and scoop out the egg yolks.

When the crust is done, she adds the filling. She makes a thick layer of red cherries, then cheesecake filling, then more red cherries, and then more cheesecake filling.

"I love red and white stripe pie," I tell her.

"What a terrific name for my pie!" she exclaims. "From now on, that's what I'll call it. Red and White Stripe Pie."

I'm all done with the eggs. Momma's all done with the pie. But we have lots of things on our list! We have more to do.

"Can we make Daddy's favorite next?" I ask.

Momma says, "That's my plan."

Daddy's favorite is brownies. Momma gets started. She puts the cocoa, flour, eggs, sugar, and butter in a bowl.

"Can I please stir the brownies?" I ask.

Handing me a long wooden spoon, Momma says, "Yes, you can stir. Stirring is a good job for you." Then she adds, "When we're done, that dog better not have any chocolate on his face. Not everyone wants to share a spoon with him!"

Ugly Brother whines under the table. I feel so sorry for him. All morning, I have been nibbling tasty food. Momma does not like Ugly Brother to eat people food, but Daddy, T.J., and I are always sneaking him treats.

We pour the brownies into a big baking pan and slide them into the oven.

Then Momma and I start cleaning up the kitchen.

Somehow, a mysterious boiled egg winds up on the floor, making one happy doggie snack for Ugly Brother. He gobbles it down in one huge bite. Then he licks his lips in case he missed any.

Chapter Eight
4th of July Jubilee

When we get up on Saturday morning, it is
hot enough to fry an egg on the sidewalk. After
a quick breakfast of cold cereal we all start to get
ready to go to the Jubilee.

Momma fries the chicken. The hot grease pops
in the skillet as she drops the chicken pieces in.
Daddy helps Momma by packing everything in
our big brown picnic basket. T.J. finds the ice chest
in the garage and loads it with ice. I get to carry
the jug of sweet tea.

Once everything is ready, we all pile into the van. But as Daddy pulls out of the driveway, I notice that we forgot something important!

"Stop this van! Where's Ugly Brother?" I shout.

Daddy stops. I jump out. Ugly Brother is chasing the van. He's dragging the bag with my glitter girl outfit in it.

"Oh, Ugly Brother, you saved me! I really forgot two things!" I cry. Then I give him the biggest squeezy hug ever.

He wags his little tail. Then we all pile back into the van and we are off to Pecan Park for the fun.

It takes about fifteen minutes to get there. When we get to the park, I spy Pappy waving at us.

Pappy has a great spot picked out under a gigantic oak tree. It is the perfect shady spot. Daddy parks the van nearby so we can unload our picnic basket, blankets, and chairs.

Our spot is at the top of the hill. We can see everything! The playground, gazebo, craft tents, and lake are below us. I bet Granny is selling her jewelry in the craft tent.

Momma and Daddy are spreading out an old red-and-white striped quilt. Momma says, "Kylie Jean, run on down to the craft tent and tell Granny we'll come look when we get our picnic blanket set up."

I shrug. "Okay, Momma."

Then I run down the hill. When I get to the tent, it doesn't take me long to find Granny.

Lots of ladies are looking at her jewelry. Earrings, bracelets, and necklaces are spread out on a long table.

I sneak up behind Granny's table and give her a big hug.

I ask, "Did you sell the bracelet I made yet?"

She smiles. "I sold it right away!" she says. "It was a big hit."

"Momma says she'll come look once the picnic is set up," I report.

"I was just fixin' to head up there myself," Granny tells me. "Will you come with me?"

I nod. Granny sets a out a little sign that says "Be Back Soon." Then she takes my hand and we walk through the tent together. I peek at the other crafts as we walk through.

"Granny, I like some of this jewelry, but yours is the best," I say. "You make the prettiest bracelets in the whole wide world."

"Why, thank you, sugar," she says. A big smile hops onto her face.

Together, we walk up the hill. We get there just in time. Momma is unloading delicious food from the brown basket.

When she lifts out the big platter of deviled eggs, I squeal.

"Look, Granny!" I say. "I made your eggs! Momma helped me a little."

Granny smiles. "I have to say, I do make fantastic deviled eggs!" she says. "I bet yours are just as good."

Daddy laughs. "I hope you made extra, Kylie Jean," he says. "T.J. and I can eat a dozen all by ourselves."

I look around at all of the colorful quilts and picnic cloths spread out in the park around the big white gazebo. The picnics look like little happy islands of people. My best cousin, Lucy, is over by the creek with her momma and daddy and her big sister, Lilly. I wave at Lucy. She waves back at me.

Ugly Brother sits beside me, licking his nose. He smells that fried chicken.

"Not yet," I tell him. "We gotta wait till Momma is ready. How about I sing my song to you?"

He barks, "Ruff."

That means no. He is tired of hearing The Star-Spangled Banner.

Crossing my arms over my chest, I mutter, "I want you to know that even though you just hurt my feelings, I still love you. And I'm ready for the talent show anyway."

T.J. pats Ugly Brother. "You put up with a lot, so don't let her push you around," T.J. tells him.

Ugly Brother barks, "Ruff, ruff!"

Sometimes, my brothers gang up on me!

Finally, Momma says, "Let's eat!"

Granny and Pappy sit in their lawn chairs. Daddy makes a plate for Granny. I make one for Pappy. Daddy puts extra potato salad on Granny's plate. I put extra deviled eggs on Pappy's plate. First the plates are full. Then the stomachs are full.

We eat and eat and eat. Everything is so good. But then Momma asks, "Are y'all ready for our Red and White Stripe Pie?"

Everyone groans. We are all too full, except for Daddy. He says, "Where are those brownies?"

Momma passes him the plate. He takes three. "I always have room for brownies," he says, winking at me.

The grown-ups sit around, talking. After a while, T.J. goes to play Frisbee with his friends.

Lucky for me, Lucy runs over. "Come and play horseshoes with us," she says. "We're having lots of fun."

I say, "Okay." Lucy and I hold hands and run down the hill toward the creek, where our other cousins are throwing horseshoes.

The horseshoes are heavy. We have to throw them at a stake that's stuck in the ground. Our big cousins can toss them real easily, but I have to throw them with two hands. So does Lucy. We both miss a lot, but we're having fun.

Clang, clang, clang go the horseshoes. But I keep thinking about singing my song for the talent show in the big white gazebo.

Chapter Nine

Talent Show Time

Before long, I see Momma walking over to us. She calls, "Kylie Jean, it's time to get ready!"

It's almost talent show time!

As we walk away from the horseshoes, Lucy yells, "Good luck, Kylie Jean!" I turn around and wave at her.

I see that Momma is carrying the bag with my glitter girl outfit in it. "Where am I gonna change?" I ask nervously.

"Don't worry," Momma says. "I have a plan."

I follow her to the park restrooms. But inside, I see that Momma wasn't the only one with this plan! There are girls and ladies everywhere. They are changing, putting on makeup, and fixing their hair. I see some square dancers. Their slips are really fluffy.

"Where can I change?" I ask Momma.

Pointing to a tiny open spot in the corner, Momma asks, "How about right there?"

We weave through the twirler girls with their batons, more square dancers, and past a girl with a big silver guitar.

Finally, I can see my changing spot. Momma hands over my bag. I pull everything out.

While I put on my costume, she tries to fix my hair, brushing out all the tangles. Then she hands me the headband with the stars that Cara let me borrow. It is just perfect.

At last, I'm ready.

I am wearing my glitter girl red and white striped shirt, my shorts, my glittery flip-flops, and Cara's headband. I kind of look like the flag!

Someone shouts, "Five minutes before we have to line up!"

Momma winks at me.

"We better go line up since you're all ready," she says.

We cross the park to the gazebo. Behind it is a table where the performers sign in. In front of the gazebo is the stage.

I step up to the table. "My name is Kylie Jean Carter and I'm a singer in the show," I say.

The girl working the table gives me a card with the number twenty-three on it. That's a really big number! I ask, "How many numbers are there for this talent show?"

She says, "Twenty-four. You are right before the last performer. We went by the order y'all signed up in. Did you sign up late?"

I reply, "Yes, ma'am."

I wish my number was fifteen. Fifteen is one of my luckiest numbers. My birthday is on the 15th. I like five, too, since there are five people in my family. Number twenty-three means I will have to wait a long, long time for my turn.

"Don't worry," Momma whispers. "You'll be busy watching the show. It'll be your turn before you know it."

I nod. Momma is right.

I can't take my eyes off of the performer who is going to go first. He is warming up by juggling a plate, a cup, three balls, and some red, white, and blue rings.

Pointing in his direction, I say, "He's good!"

Momma waits with me in line.

The talent show is about to start and everyone in the park moves closer to the gazebo.

That's when I start to get nervous!

Chapter Ten
Showtime!

I listen to the mayor of our town, Mr. Richardson, announce the performers.

He calls out, "Let's get this show started! Everyone, give a big hand for our first performer, Dan the Juggling Man."

I watch Dan juggle some more. He is awesome! Next, several dance groups perform. I watch tap dancers and square dancers. One of the square dancers has on a pink and white dress with a big fluffy pink slip.

I whisper, "I want to learn how to square dance."

Momma whispers back, "You just want a pink dress like that dancer has on!"

I laugh, covering my mouth. Momma sure does know me!

The magician's act is really interesting until his rabbit gets stuck in his hat. Someone in line says he should have practiced more.

He's a kid, just like me.

Lots of people cheer for the baton twirlers. They have plain batons, not the kind you light on fire.

The fiery batons would be more exciting. They are number fifteen.

I whisper to Momma, "I wish I was number fifteen, because I sure do like that number, and if I was number fifteen I'd be all done now."

Momma smiles and pats my shoulder. "It won't be long now," she says.

Number sixteen is a bunch of little girls doing gymnastics. They take lessons at Tammy's Tumbling School. They get mixed up and bump into each other.

One of them starts to cry, and her momma has to go get her off the stage in front of everyone!

Then there are more singers. A church group sings. After that, we watch more dancers.

Then there's an old man with a puppet in his lap. The puppet talks.

That doesn't make a lot of sense to me, so I ask Momma quietly, "Momma, how does the puppet talk?"

Momma says, "The puppet is called a dummy, because it can't talk. The man is doing the talking, but it sounds like it's coming from the dummy."

Finally, it's my turn. I'm nervous. I feel like I swallowed a bowl full of June bugs!

Mr. Richardson says, "Folks, up next is Kylie Jean Carter, singin' The Star-Spangled Banner."

Everyone claps as I walk to the center of the stage. I stand right in front of the microphone and then I start to sing as loud as I can.

I'm glad I practiced my song a lot. The words are easy for me now.

On my third time through, I say, "Come on, y'all! You know the song. Sing it with me!"

Everyone starts to sing. I see Lucy and Cara singing. Daddy, Granny, and everybody in my family — they're all singing too.

At the end, I tell everyone, "I just love America, so Happy Birthday to the good ole USA."

I'm pretty sure I'm gonna win it.

Then Mandy Howard comes up to sing. She's number twenty-four. She sings so pretty my heart wants to float right out of my chest. I never heard a singer with a voice as sweet as hers! That's when I realize I want Mandy to win. She deserves it.

When the judges announce the winners, third place goes to Dan the Juggling Man.

Mr. Richardson calls my name for second place. I jump up and down. Momma gives me a big squeezy hug. I look for Daddy, T.J., and Ugly Brother, but I can't see them.

Then Mr. Richardson calls out, "First place, Mandy Howard."

I shout, "Yes!"

And even though I didn't win, I am as happy as butter on a biscuit.

Chapter Eleven
Fireworks, Sparklers, and Singers

My family expects me to be sad, but I'm not sad at all. I'm glad Mandy won. She deserved it the most! Her voice was just so pretty!

"Good for you," Daddy says. "You did a wonderful job and you're not a sore loser."

"You're not a loser at all," T.J. says. He even gives me a hug!

When the sky is finally the color of black ink, the real show begins.

You know I just love the fireworks!

All around the park, sparklers blink like fireflies. About a million people are waiting for the fireworks to start. Some sit on quilts, others on the fronts of their cars.

Mr. Richardson and Mandy find me lying on my blanket in the field.

"How about a song from our Jubilee talent show winners while we wait for the fireworks to start?" Mr. Richardson asks. "You and Mandy would do a lovely duet."

That sounds so fun! I like the idea of singing again!

I look at Momma. "Can I do it?" I ask. "I really want to."

"Go ahead," Momma says. "We'll be right here."

"Okay," I say. I follow Mandy over to the piano in the gazebo.

She whispers, "Sit beside me. We'll sing America the Beautiful. You sing the America, America part. Okay?"

I wiggle with excitement. "Yup, I got it," I whisper back. Then Mandy starts to play the song and we sing.

Suddenly, it seems like a thousand voices are singing with us. Everyone in town knows the words to our song, and everyone wants to sing along. The voices blend, making a giant choir singing in the night.

Above us, the night sky explodes with electric color. The fireworks light up the gazebo as we finish our song.

Mandy and I stand together. The crowd is clapping so loud it sounds like thunder.

Mandy blows kisses. I do my beauty queen wave, nice and slow, side to side.

Even a second-place singer can sparkle like a real, true beauty queen!

Marci Bales Peschke was born in Indiana, grew up in Florida, and now lives in Texas with her husband, two children, and a feisty black-and-white cat named Phoebe. She loves reading and watching movies.

When **Tuesday Mourning** was a little girl, she knew she wanted to be an artist when she grew up. Now, she is an illustrator who lives in South Pasadena, CA. She especially loves illustrating books for kids and teenagers. When she isn't illustrating, Tuesday loves spending time with her husband, who is an actor, and their two sons.

Glossary

banner (BAN-ur)—a long piece of material with writing, pictures, or a design on it

concentrate (KON-suhn-trate)—think hard and carefully

costume (KOSS-toom)—clothes worn for a certain event

jubilee (joo-buh-LEE)—a big celebration to mark the anniversary of a special event

opinion (uh-PIN-yuhn)—ideas and beliefs about something

patriotic (pay-tree-OT-ik)—having love for your country

spangled (SPAYNG-uhld)—sparkling

talent (TAL-uhnt)—a natural ability or skill

talented (TAL-uhnt-id)—very good at something

usual (YOO-zhoo-uhl)—normal

verse (VURSS)—one part of a poem or song

Talk!

1. Kylie Jean didn't win. So why wasn't she sad? Talk about your answer.

2. Kylie Jean gets help from many people in this book. Who do you get help from? How do those people help you?

3. What do you think happens after this story ends? Talk about it!

Be Creative!

1. Kylie Jean's goal is to be a beauty queen. What's your number-one dream?

2. Who is your favorite character in this story? Draw a picture of that person. Then write a list of five things you know about them.

3. What if you were in a talent show? Write about your best talent!

This is a perfect summer picnic treat! Make sure you have a grown-up to help you melt the candy topping.

Love, Kylie Jean

From Momma's Kitchen

RED, WHITE, AND BLUE JUBILEE POPS

YOU NEED:

1 package of sandwich cookies (the kind with extra filling is the best!)

Red, white, and blue candy melts

Red, white, and blue sprinkles

A package of lollipop sticks

A grown-up helper

Waxed paper

1. Carefully stick a lollipop stick into the filling of each cookie. Place the pops on a cookie sheet and refrigerate 15 minutes.

2. Ask your grown-up helper to melt the candy melts and put each color in its own glass container. Be careful—this is hot! Line a cookie sheet with waxed paper.

3. Dip each cookie pop into one color. Sprinkle with sprinkles and place on waxed-paper-lined cookie sheet. Move quickly so that the candy doesn't harden too fast. If your candy gets too hard, ask your helper to re-melt it. Cool cookie pops in refrigerator for 10 minutes before serving. Yum, yum!

Kylie Jean

has one BIG dream . . .
to be a beauty queen!

Available from Picture Window Books
www.capstonepub.com

THE FUN DOESN'T STOP HERE!

Discover more at www.capstonekids.com

- ♥ Videos & Contests
- ✿ Games & Puzzles
- ♥ Friends & Favorites
- ✿ Authors & Illustrators

Find cool websites and more books like this one at www.facthound.com. Just type in the Book ID: **9781404868007** and you're ready to go!